The Best Mummy Snails in the whole wide world

By Troy Jenkinson

For Emma, Jo, Grace and Evie

Orchard House Publishing. Printed in Ibstock, Leicestershire, UK

There were once two African Snails named Felicity and Jane. They were both very smiley snails who loved one another's company very much. Everywhere that Felicity slithered, Jane slithered too. They were quite inseparable.

Felicity loved Jane very much.
She thought that the patterns on Jane's
shell were the most beautiful patterns
she had ever seen. Jane loved Felicity
very much too. She loved to look at
Felicity's sparkly eyes on her
slender tentacles.

One day, Jane slithered towards Felicity
with great news. She was going to
have some baby snails. Jane was so
excited that she didn't notice the smile
appear on Felicity's mouth. Felicity
too was going to have some babies.
The two ecstatic snails were going to
become mummies.

6

The two snails worked hard together to build their egg chamber. They dug in the soil together and soon they had the perfect chamber to lay their eggs. Side by side Felicity and Jane sat, pleased with their efforts.

Carefully, very carefully, they laid their eggs together in the chamber. As the last egg was laid, Jane began to cover the eggs in the soft soil to keep them safe. Felicity smiling helped. Now all they had to do was wait.

It wasn't long before Felicity and Jane heard the tiniest noises coming from within the egg chamber. The first of their baby snails hatched from the eggs. Felicity was desperate to meet their new babies but Jane reminded her that they needed to let them come out of the egg chamber by themselves. They needed to keep safe and warm until they were ready to meet their mums.

They didn't have to wait very long at all. Felicity, who had been tending the egg chamber every day since they covered the clutch of eggs was the first to spot a baby's tentacle peeking through the soft soil. Jane slithered over so they could both see their first baby as he emerged from the chamber.

Felicity and Jane proudly smiled as the baby snail came fully into view. The nepionic whorls on his newly formed shell were stunning. Felicity turned to Jane with a knowing smile that meant 'He looks just like you.' They named him Frank.

Soon another tentacle appeared.
Frank was joined by his baby brother,
Karl. Felicity and Jane had never had
such enormous smiles.

Now they had two gorgeous baby snails to tend and care for. They brought them delicious green leaves to munch on so they could grow big and strong.

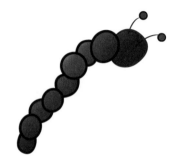

And big and strong they became.
Slithering after their mummies they
went, Frank and Karl were a delightful
pair of brothers. No mummy snail could
have been prouder.

So next time you see two snails smiling
at you together in the soil, ask yourself,
is this Felicity and Jane? They are
the best mummy snails in the
whole wide world!